ONCE UPON MY DADS' DIVORCE

BY **Seamus Kirst**

ILLUSTRATED BY **Noémie Gionet Landry**

MAGINATION PRESS · WASHINGTON, DC
AMERICAN PSYCHOLOGICAL ASSOCIATION

To anyone finding a new normal—SK.

To Maude, Laurent and Grégoire-My happily ever after—NGL

Books for Kids From the
American Psychological Association

Magination Press is a registered trademark of the American Psychological Association.
Order books at maginationpress.org, or call 1-800-374-2721.

Book design by Christina Gaugler
Printed by LakeBook Manufacturing LLC, Melrose Park, IL

Library of Congress Cataloging-in-Publication Data
Names: Kirst, Seamus, author. | Gionet Landry, Noémie, illustrator.
Title: Once upon my dads' divorce / by Seamus Kirst ; illustrated by Noémie Gionet Landry.
Description: Washington, DC : Magination Press, [2023] | "American Psychological Association."
Summary: After his two fathers divorce, Grayson goes from one house with both parents to splitting his time
between his Papa's apartment and his Daddy's house.
Identifiers: LCCN 2023006612 | ISBN 9781433840746 (hardback) | ISBN 9781433840753 (ebook)
Subjects: CYAC: Divorce—Fiction. | Gay fathers—Fiction. | Family life—Fiction. | LCGFT: Picture books.
Classification: LCC PZ7.1.K626 On 2023 | DDC [E]—dc23
LC record available at https://lccn.loc.gov/2023006612

Manufactured in the United States of America

10 9 8 7 6 5 4 3 2 1

Once upon a time,

I lived in a big brick house
with Papa and Daddy...

...with a swing set
in the backyard,

a big bedroom with
a midnight sky and
planets and stars,

a cozy kitchen where we made banana chocolate chip pancakes on Saturdays,

and a comfy bed where I read happily ever after fairy tales with Papa and Daddy every night!

But in my story, there is no wicked witch or big bad wolf.

Instead, the villain is...

DIVORCE!

Ever since that day,
everything's been different.

First, Papa moved into an apartment.

Next, Daddy moved into a smaller house.

Then we sold the big brick house.

Before we left our big brick house,
I emptied out my drawers and took
my favorite dinosaur picture off the wall.

I divided up my clothes and toys. I had to
keep half of each at both of the new places.

It was so hard!

Now, I split my time between
Papa's apartment and Daddy's house!

It's one week with Papa...

Then one week with Daddy.

Every Saturday night, I packed up a small suitcase and my backpack before heading to the other place.

I had to be extra careful not to leave anything that I'd need that week behind.

"This is the new normal," said Papa.

Well it feels like a nightmare, I thought.

"I know it's hard, but you will get used to it," said Daddy.

Now that I just didn't believe.

Week after week passed,
and it didn't feel easier.

I felt like I left half of myself
at Papa's and half of myself
at Daddy's.

Why can't Papa and Daddy just stay married? I wondered. We could still live happily ever after.

I tried not to let my mind wander to sad places, but sometimes I couldn't help it.

*What if they got divorced
because of me?*

Weeks turned into months.

Back and forth I went.

At Papa's
apartment,
I didn't have my
favorite books.

At Daddy's
house, I didn't
have my old bed.

And neither place felt like my real home!

One Saturday night, Papa called, "Grayson, it's time to pack up so I can take you to Daddy's house."

I hid.

"Grayson!" Papa kept calling. "Where are you?"

I heard him check the bathroom. I heard him open the closet door.

Finally, he looked under the bed.

"What are you doing?" Papa asked.

"I'm not going to Daddy's house," I cried. "I'm not coming out until you, me, and Daddy go back to live at the old house."

"I'm sorry you're so upset," said Papa. "I'll take you to see the old house. First, let me make a quick call."

I crawled out from under the bed
and grabbed my suitcase.

Papa drove me to our old house.

Daddy was standing by his car, parked out front.

"Daddy," I called, running to him. "I want to move back here with you and Papa!"

Daddy gave me a big hug. "We can't move back in, Grayson," he said.

"We are getting divorced," said Papa, "and that means we have to live in separate places."

"Are you getting divorced because of something I did?!"
I asked. "I will do anything if we can all be together, again."

"Oh, Grayson," said Papa.
"You are the best thing that
ever happened to both of us."

"None of this is your fault," said Daddy.
"We are getting divorced because we both
are different than we were when we got married."

"Not different in a bad way," said Papa.
"But different in a way that makes us know
we will both be happier if we don't stay married."

"But I'm not happier!" I said.

"Moving back into the old house won't fix what's making you sad," said Papa. "I don't think it's our old house you want back, it's our old way of life."

"Grayson, we know everything has changed and that it's been very hard," said Daddy. "But even though you live in new places and Papa and I are getting divorced, you are still you."

"I'm still the same Papa," said Papa.
"Daddy is still the same Daddy."

"We both still love you," said Daddy.
"We always will."

"So we are still a family," I said.
"Just a different kind of family."

Papa and Daddy hugged me.
I hugged them back.

I started to believe Papa and Daddy that one day happily ever after would still happen after all.

Reader's Note

by Julia Martin Burch, PhD

Divorce is hard on all members of a family. Separating parents must cope with a range of painful emotions around the experience, as well as navigate the many challenges involved in separating a household and establishing two new ones. Children can have many different reactions to divorce as well. Some feel angry and resentful and act out, others can withdraw and isolate, while still others may worry that they caused the divorce, as Grayson does in the story. Though divorce is an undeniably challenging experience for children to face, there is much the adults in their lives can do to support them and help them navigate this difficult time.

Communicate

Clear, accurate, and calm communication is a cornerstone of supporting children through a divorce. When you share information with your child about the divorce or the plans for your future households, be as concrete and specific as you can. Strive to find a balance between keeping your child aware of events and plans, while also not sharing more than is developmentally appropriate. Resist the urge to overpromise things that may not happen, such as moving into a specific new house or spending more time with your former partner than is realistic to expect. Though it is tempting to make optimistic promises to help your child feel better in the moment, your child will only feel more unsettled and upset if those promises do not come to pass. Across all communications with your child,

look for opportunities to reassure them that the divorce is not their fault and that you and your former partner both love them very much.

Be an Effective Co-Parent

Even if there is tension between you and your former partner, do your best to be collaborative co-parents. Communicate directly with them rather than through your child. Speak about them respectfully and treat them with civility in front of your child. Resist the urge to share adult-level details around why the divorce is occurring. Children deserve the chance to have a loving relationship with both of their parents. When you share critical information about your former partner, it puts your child in the middle and can make them feel as though they must choose a side. Work together to the best of your abilities to insulate your child from any adult conflict.

Be Consistent

Children thrive with predictability and consistency. Accordingly, one of the many factors that makes divorce difficult for kids is the upending of their routines. Do your best to maintain your child's routines and to keep their life feeling normal. When you must change a routine, establish a new one promptly and try to stick with it. It can be helpful to use child-friendly visual prompts, like the calendar in the story or a picture checklist of what to pack for each parent's house. Similarly, stay consistent with

behavioral expectations for your child. It can be tempting to relax the normal rules when your child is upset, but this tends to backfire by making the world feel even more unpredictable. Keep day to day life consistent to help your child develop a sense of stability in their new situation.

Stay Involved

Do your best to prioritize time with your child, particularly through the busy early days of the divorce and household transitions. Your presence is stabilizing to your child when it feels like their world has been upended. This time does not need to involve grand gestures or expense. Instead, strive to just connect with your child and to do things they enjoy together. Similarly, be supportive of the time your child spends with their other parent. No matter how you feel towards your former partner, do your best to support their ability to maintain a relationship with your child.

Listen and Validate

Routinely ask your child how they are feeling. No matter how they respond, strive to listen openly and nonjudgmentally. For example, saying "I can understand why you would feel that way. Can you tell me more?" shows your child that you accept their feelings and want to understand their experience. Relatedly, resist any urges to "fix" the emotions they are feeling or to cheer them up. Though this is well intended, doing so can put pressure on your child to feel a way that they don't feel or

send the message that their emotions are just a problem to be solved.

Let them know that they won't hurt your feelings with what they say. Make sure you are using your own coping tools to stay calm and supportive in these conversations, even if your child says something that is hard for you to hear. Get support if you need it to be sure you can remain calm and collected with your child. Reassure your child that, no matter how painful their feelings are, they will eventually find a new equilibrium.

When to Seek Support

As discussed, it is normal for children to experience a range of emotions and reactions in response to a divorce. However, if you have concerns about the intensity of your child's distress or if you notice that their functioning has been impacted (for example, withdrawing from previously enjoyed activities) it may be helpful to consult with a mental health professional who specializes in working with children.

Julia Martin Burch, PhD, *is a clinical psychologist in private practice. She specializes in evidence-based treatments, including cognitive behavior therapy and exposure and response prevention therapy for youth anxiety, obsessive compulsive, and related disorders. She completed her training at Fairleigh Dickinson University and Massachusetts General Hospital/ Harvard Medical School.*

Seamus Kirst is a writer whose work has been published in *The Washington Post*, *The New York Times*, *The Guardian*, *Teen Vogue*, *Forbes*, *The Advocate*, and *Vice*. He is the author of *Papa, Daddy, and Riley* and *Dad and Daddy's Big Big Family*. He lives in Brooklyn, NY. Visit @SeamusPatrickKirst on Facebook and @SeamusKirst on Instagram.

Noémie Gionet Landry shares her time between the hospital where she works as a rheumatologist and her home studio where she sketches, draws, and paints. She is the illustrator of the acclaimed books *Bailey the Bat and the Tangled Moose* and *The Monster Parade: A Book about Feeling All Your Feelings and Then Watching Them Go*. She lives in New Brunswick, Canada. Visit noemiegionetlandry.squarespace.com and @noemie_illustration on Instagram.

Magination Press is the children's book imprint of the American Psychological Association. APA works to advance psychology as a science and profession and as a means of promoting health and human welfare. Magination Press books reach young readers and their parents and caregivers to make navigating life's challenges a little easier. It's the combined power of psychology and literature that makes a Magination Press book special. Visit maginationpress.org and @MaginationPress on Facebook, Twitter, Instagram, and Pinterest.